What Women Are Saying About This Book...

I thoroughly enjoyed this book; the stories are amazing and made me laugh.
Actually, I think I've dated Ned myself.
—DEBBIE, KANSAS CITY

Therapeutic for those who have "been there," a must read for those who haven't.
—HOLLY, SAN DIEGO

Humorous, serious, informative, but, most of all, real.
—BOBBIE, WISCONSIN

Thanks for validating some of my own experiences—I thought it was just me.
—REBECCA, SEATTLE

The very reason why I always carry my cellular phone and have money for cab fare.
—PAM, NEW YORK

Illustration by Mark A. Cerny

LOSERS, CREEPS, JERKS & WEIRDOS

A Dating Story

Cynthia P. Cerny

PN 6231 .D3 C47 2002
Cerny, Cynthia P.
Losers, creeps, jerks &
 weirdos

HRH
Classics

Losers, Creeps, Jerks, and Weirdos: A Dating Story
is a work of nonfiction, based on the dating experiences of the
author. In consideration of the actual persons depicted, names
and locations have been changed.

Published by HRH Classics
Post Office Box 261393
Highlands Ranch, Colorado 80163-1393

Visit our web site at *www.HRHClassics.com*

Library of Congress Control Number 2002107350

ISBN 0-9721463-1-8

Cover and interior design: Michele DeFilippo, 1106 Design
Author photograph by Darrell Pierson of BodyPhotage

Manufactured in the United States of America

Dedication

To my extraordinary parents,
Rita and John Cerny,
who have always believed, always supported,
and, most importantly,
always been there.

Yours is a true love story;
and to think it all started with a blind date
over 45 years ago.
May I be as lucky.

My love and gratitude,

—CYNTHIA

Contents

Acknowledgments

The idea for this book was originally proposed to me by my best friend, Roxann Wamsat-Bohling, who, after I endured a particularly lousy lot of dates, told me "You should write a book; who would ever believe that someone like you could run into so many losers?" So, Roxann, here it is. You were a steadfast sounding board and thoughtful ear for all my post-date analyses; you know these stories as well as I. There is simply no better friend. And to your husband, Ken, thank you for letting me borrow Roxann for "girl talk" even when that meant the occasional phone call at a less than agreeable hour (we won't even mention duration!).

Even with the seed planted, this book required the support, assistance, and timely encouragement of many. To my now late-grandmother Alice Clink Schumacher, an accomplished author, poet, and speaker, consider this book a promise kept.

To Professor Martin Marshall, Harvard School of Business, thank you for prodding me from start to finish. I'll always cherish the note you wrote that simply read: "No excuses; make time for your writing. I will expect to see an updated manuscript soon."

To Leslie Lundberg, thank you for your friendship, feedback, and faith. You will never know how much it meant to me when even my earliest, roughest draft made you laugh.

To accomplished authors John T. Reed and Christina Adam, thank you for generously sharing your time and wealth of experience. Your input changed my entire direction and approach.

To Cheryl Butler, your reaction has made me believe I have "hit the mark." Thank you. You are a dear friend.

To Rick Adam, my deepest gratitude for your overwhelming support. To Pat Fortune, who doesn't understand the happy dance, but who did teach me about entertainment value, thank you. To Ray Vinton, Terry Truman, and John Magee, whose support, guidance, and willingness to help simply left me speechless. Your generosity is awe-inspiring.

To my brother Mark who is simply the best brother a sister could ever hope for. Thank you for lending your talents to my book.

To my personal heroes, my Mom and Dad. You are my strength. I am truly blest to have you in my corner.

And, finally, to Grizz…you know.

The
Bachelorette

L et's begin by meeting the bachelorette. Victoria is a fun-loving spark of energy at 5-foot, 5-inches tall; 110 pounds; with light brown shoulder-length hair; green eyes; and great smile to complement her optimistic, cheerful attitude. Think "perky," "sporty," or "cute," and you have a picture of Victoria.

Her interests are well-versed and include golfing, biking, dancing, reading, traveling, evening walks, and lengthy dinners with friends. Especially, lengthy dinners with friends! Independent and hardworking, Victoria lives a secure life-style, having successfully provided for herself the material comforts some women are not able to experience without the financial contributions of a partner. With strong family ties, good friends, her own home, reliable transportation, a growing nest egg, and very little "baggage," Victoria doesn't need a man to "rescue her" or "complete her." She is a whole female person looking for a whole male person to share the simple joy of mutual interest and companionship. Straightforward and uncomplicated. To those who know her, Victoria is a "good catch."

For the naïve or rookie single, the story would go something like this… Smart, attractive, financially secure female dates equally intelligent, eye-pleasing, successful men. Has a few sub par dates then finds her man. They marry and the rest is statistics. For the veteran singles, we know better. For the rest of you—wake up, the coffee is burning.

The truth of the matter is, losers, creeps, jerks, and weirdos are running amuck in the dating world. Strategically sprinkled across the land, you are bound to have your own personal encounter of the bizarre-o kind. Don't be fooled, cleverly disguised, these XY chromosomes often appear as sophisticated, successful, honorable persons. Yes, there are still good guys available, but you're probably going to have to get a big shovel and dig deep.

Now, ladies, put away your archeological tools, pour yourself a glass of wine, sit back, turn the page, and know that you're in good company. X

Liar,
Liar,
Pants
on Fire

To say that Ned had a difficult time with the truth would be like saying penguins have difficulty flying. Penguins have wings, can't fly. Ned had a voice, couldn't speak the truth. Thankfully, I figured this out before I invested too much time.

I met Ned at work; dating a coworker was a mistake unto itself. Ned was tall and slender with boyish good looks. Charming, confident, and impeccably dressed he could have just as easily walked off the pages of *GQ*. Ned was in sales, which, of course, was the perfect profession for his personality type and particular character weakness. He was a mere three years older than I, but he seemed light years ahead in sophistication and worldly matters. The key word here, ladies, is "seemed"—Ned was the King of Deception—a big, fat liar.

Of course there are two sides to every story; so for those of you who may be inclined to come to Ned's defense thinking I'm being overly harsh, have poor communication skills, or lack the ability to comprehend English sufficiently, allow me to submit into evidence the following examples. Then you decide.

It was just after 7 p.m. on a Thursday when I telephoned Ned to see if he would be interested in catching the 8:30 p.m. movie. A sexy, breathy female voice answers:

"Hello?"

I immediately apologize for having misdialed and hang up. I check the number and carefully redial. Same voice, same greeting.

"Hello?"

"Is this 555-9318?"

"Yes."

"I'm calling for Ned. Who is this?"

"Who is this?"

I feel my face warming and my heart begins to beat just a little faster. I take a deep breath.

"This is Victoria...his girlfriend."

There is silence and then a muffled voice in the background. Words are being exchanged, but I can't hear them clearly enough to understand. I continue.

"Hello!...hello!...may I please speak to Ned?!?!"

The line disconnects. With the worst possible thoughts racing through my mind, I call back. Ned answers on the first ring.

"Ned, who was that on the phone?"

"No one, just my cleaning lady."

Now let's pause here and think. I guess this could have been true if:

1. Ned's apartment was actually ever clean.
2. I had called between 8 a.m. and 5 p.m. (This maid, it seemed, preferred the night shift.)
3. She had answered the phone more like household help actually screening calls and less like Bambi, sex line bimbo.

I had a lot of questions, but Ned was deflecting them left and right. He was relentless in trying to shift the spotlight on me, accusing me of being childish, jealous, and having poor phone manners. Sure, that was the problem, *my* poor phone etiquette. The argument went nowhere. A sign of things to come...

Want to label it a mistake, a misunderstanding? Okay, what about this one...

A holiday weekend was approaching and I really wanted to get away from the city. Ned suggested we spend a few days at a spa resort a scenic three-hour drive away. He handled all of the arrangements and spared no expense—from the penthouse suite to wonderful spa treatments to a $300 bottle of wine with dinner—everything was just so. Well, at least until it came time to check out.

Presented with the four-figure bill, Ned casually presented his Gold AMEX. Denied. Platinum Visa. Denied. Gold MasterCard. Denied. Discover card. They didn't accept Discover. Different Visa. Denied.

The only credit card that worked was mine, and it was the only way we were going to get out of there without having to bus tables or tourists.

On the ride home, Ned was a talking book of excuses, pointing the finger at everything and anyone but himself. "Computer glitch" was his brilliant conclusion. Not to worry, though, Ned promised to pay me back. Of course, we broke up before hell froze over so I never did collect on that debt.

Before you cast your final vote—"big fat liar" or "misunderstood male"—here is one last example for your consideration.

We had just reached the two-month dating mark when I met the maid-of-honor-to-be at Ned's wedding-to-be. Say what? It turns out that Ned had just broken off his engagement to his long-time girlfriend. Long-time girlfriend? Engagement? Wait a minute…we had talked about this. He claimed to have been "girlfriend-less" for over a year. I gave his excuse 1 out of 5 stars—it had more holes in it than a moth-infested sweater and lacked his usual creativity.

The cleaning lady, the computer glitch, and, now, the engagement—it was exhausting sifting through all his stories to find the "sliver of truth," not to mention annoying and not the type of character I wanted to be around. It was time to chalk one up to experience. Just one more item of business—I confronted Ned. I wanted to know why it was seemingly impossible for him to be open, direct, and truthful. His response?

"I knew if I had been honest with you from the start you would have never gone out with me."

Now *that,* boys and girls, is the truth, and the truth shall set you free! ▧

The
Fix-Up

Joel was a blind date set up by my friend, Amy, and her husband, Russ. Russ and Joel were best buddies. We decided to make the evening a double date and go dancing. Normally I dreaded blind dates, but how bad could this be? After all, it was friends introducing friends…

It was a summer evening and the parking lot was nearly full when I arrived at the upscale restaurant and dance hall. I found the threesome waiting for me at a table near the bar. After introductions, Amy and Russ quickly excused themselves, allowing Joel and I time to get acquainted. Unlike most of my previous dating experiences, the conversation was a struggle. Joel seemed distracted and distant; there were breaks in the dialogue to rival the Grand Canyon. After what seemed an eternity Amy and Russ returned to the table and Joel became Mr. Talkative, bragging about his work as a police officer. Problem was Joel wasn't on the force; he wasn't even mall security. In reality, where I like to live most of the time, Joel was working temporary jobs while deciding on a career path. Nothing wrong with that unless you lie about it (probably a friend of Ned's). Strike 1.

We had been sitting for about 30 minutes when Russ asked Joel if he had offered to buy me a drink. "No," came the flat reply "I didn't bring any money." He didn't bring any money on a date? What kind of idiot was this? Inconsiderate...Strike 2. Russ purchased the meal and drinks for the evening. I couldn't believe it. One thing is sure, no one can accuse me of going after a sugar daddy. After 20 minutes of small talk, Russ prodded Joel to ask me to dance. So we did...kind of. The dance experience would have had a chance for success had Joel actually dedicated some level of concentration to the music, his feet, and the other couples within our immediate dance space. Instead, it was like roller derby without the skates; Joel was tripping over his feet, stepping on my feet, and not exactly looking out for others. After two dances I had had enough. Safely off the dance floor, Joel and I returned to our table where painful solitude and police wannabe stories continued. And all this without an alcoholic refreshment to dull the senses. Next thing I know, Joel started conversing with a group of ladies seated at the table next to ours. For the next ten minutes my only view of Joel was the back of his head. Rude...Strike 3. One more chance at bat, I thought to myself. I looked at my watch, not quite an hour had passed. It was going to be a long night.

As Amy and Russ once again returned to the table, Joel, who was painfully oblivious to my existence by this time, stood up and escorted one of the gals from the neighboring table onto the dance floor. When Joel returned only to exchange women, I had reached the boiling point. Strike 1, 2, 3 and 4...I was outta there.

I gathered my coat, waved good-bye to Amy and Russ, and headed toward the exit. Joel dashed off the floor and pleaded with me to stay. He explained that he had just felt sorry that "those women" were without dates. He explained that he was a bit insecure and didn't always make a good first impression.

"I'm really a nice guy. Let's talk. I know you might think I've been a jerk, but I really don't think it's been an evening we can't repair."

Honey, even Sears doesn't make enough tools to repair what happened on this date. Here was a guy who, being well-aware he was going out on a date, left his wallet home; was hallucinatory about what he did for a living; and somehow mistook me for being a triplet. I think this has "jerk" written all over it.

Amy called the next morning to apologize on Joel's behalf (I guess dialing the phone was too challenging for him). We were able to find the entertainment value in it all and she assured me that Joel's path and mine would not "accidentally" cross again.

Five months later, under the guise that time heals all, Amy called to let me know Joel was inquiring about the possibility of a second date. She explained that Joel had told her how he had changed. "Great," I said "who is he now?" ■

Desperado

Jake was a friend of a friend. We had first met a year earlier at a party, but I didn't recall the introduction. On the contrary Jake was able to accurately describe everything I was wearing that evening, down to my jewelry.

Jake had learned through this friend of a friend that I was "available" and, with my permission, was provided my telephone number. We spoke over the phone several times before our date. The dialogue wasn't particularly free-flowing or lively, but it wasn't so bad as to make it a date breaker. I figured he just wasn't a phone kind of guy. We set the date for Friday night. He would pick me up at 7 p.m. and my attire should be dressy casual.

The door bell rang promptly at 7 p.m. So far the guy was observant *and* prompt (two points—for those keeping score). He was dressed in slacks, a turtleneck, and sport coat. I had opted for slacks and a sweater. He helped me with my coat and we were on our way.

Jake had made dinner reservations at a fabulous mountain-top restaurant located approximately 35-minutes outside of town—for normal drivers.

A 60-minute commute if your name is Jake. He helped me up and into his SUV of which the new car smell signaled that it was a very recent purchase. When I commented about this Jake replied, "Yeah, my daughters finally convinced me that my previous car was a date killer. They thought this would attract more women." (Okay, scorekeepers, subtract one point.)

As we continued along our route to the restaurant it quickly became apparent that Jake's choice of vehicle wasn't his only problem. He was an absolute disaster behind the wheel. He drove at a speed that would barely challenge a crawling toddler, but that wasn't the worst...he used the lane marker as a centering point and came to a dead stop in the passing lane mistaking it for a left turn lane. By now, I had checked and re-checked my seatbelt a half dozen times and my right hand was gripping the door handle so tight I nearly stopped the blood flow. I was abnormally happy (read "thankful") when we finally reached the restaurant. "Can I get you something to drink?" our waiter inquired. Can you ever! (Scorekeepers may stop scoring; we reached negative double-digit points on the roadway.)

With cocktail in hand, wine ordered, I was beginning to relax again and the conversation commenced. If opposites attract Jake and I should have been all over each other. I'm a fitness fanatic; he was a couch potato. He was a walking encyclopedia of movies and entertainers; I couldn't recall the last time I had been at the cinema. I am not—to put it nicely—a cat person; he had four. His favorite vacation spot was my least favorite. Are you seeing a trend here? As much as we probed we had *nothing* in common. The food was wonderful, the wine fabulous, the setting beautiful, and the conversation had just enough life to keep it off a respirator.

The drive back was another "white knuckler," but the alcohol had done it's job—I didn't care. Well I thought, as we neared my house, at least this one is mutual. We will say a polite good-bye and go our very separate ways. Pulling into the driveway, Jake asked if he could come in. During dinner I had mentioned that I was writing a novel and he wanted to read a chapter. Okay, no harm in that.

Jake settled on the couch and I pulled the shortest chapter I could find for him to read. When he finished he looked at me and said, "Wow! This is really very good. I can't believe I am dating an author." Now, if that didn't make my heart melt a bit. I looked at him again. Was I missing something?

As I walked Jake to the door he turned and said, "I had a great time. I want to kiss you, but I just got rid of a cold and don't want to risk spreading the germs. Let's go out again next weekend…what do you say?" Okay, I wasn't expecting this. Did he not see we shared no common ground? Was this the same guy that sat across from me at dinner? Why would he want to waste his time? As my mind searched on for answers my mouth opened and the words "Sure. Fine." fell out.

The following week was my birthday and Jake sent me two dozen roses and a balloon bouquet large enough to cause lift-off of my desk. The card read "Happy birthday to my favorite author! Looking forward to Saturday night!" And the gifts didn't stop there. Every other day a package would arrive with a note referencing our upcoming date. It was overkill and it was making me very uncomfortable. We weren't a match. The more we talked the wider the gap became and that's when it hit me…he was Mr. Desperado. Time to put the horse back in the barn.

I telephoned Jake at home that evening. I was quite anxious; breaking up is not my forté. Here was a nice guy who deserved a great lady. And here was a nice lady who deserved a great guy. We were just the wrong nice people for each other. How do you say that without hurting the other person's feelings; without them thinking it's a line? Speak from the heart, speak slowly and softly, and speak with kindness. Ready, set, go!

"Hello, Jake, it's Victoria. I'm a bit nervous so bear with me. I want to be upfront with you. I think you're a terrific guy and you deserve someone just as terrific. As we've talked the past few weeks it has become increasingly obvious to me that we don't share much in common. I know you are looking for a long-term relationship and I just don't want to waste your time or mine. I think we should cancel our plans for Saturday night. I'm sorry."

(The pause of eternity)

"Okay, thanks for calling. (Click)"

Ouch! I spent the next few hours analyzing our entire relationship of a half dozen phone calls and one dinner. What could I have done different? Was I too harsh? Too quick to judge? Too…??? Why was I tearing myself apart over this? It wasn't a crime that things didn't work out. Where was my testosterone? I doubt that Jake was doing any self-analysis and I'll bet the farm he didn't lose one minute of sleep. In situations like this, it helps to handle them like a man. ☒

Run,
Baby,
Run!

Run, Baby, Run! Ladies, why is it when such words are spoken by a male we don't heed the warning? Worse yet, we act as if it's some supersonic mating call. Our heart, being the lousy translator it is, hears "He really wants me. I'm good for him. I'll open his eyes." Big, BIG mistake!

Dave was the guy who told me to run away after our third date. Date No. 1 consisted of dinner and conversation in an interview-like format. We discovered we had many things in common and the laughter came easily. Date No. 2 was a picnic in the park and shooting hoops. We found we shared similar long-term goals. Date No. 3 was golf. Even the stodgy country club atmosphere could not deter our laughter or enthusiasm for the great time we were experiencing together. So in the parking lot when Dave swung me around to face him eye-to-eye and these words spilled out, it was easier to let my heart play interpreter than allow my brain to acknowledge the big red flag flapping in my face.

One year after that day in the parking lot I finally "got it" and canned the interpreter. What Dave knew to be true after our third date was that I deserved better than what he was willing to offer. Had I employed my head rather than my heart it could have saved us both a lot of grief. Instead, I trudged through months of conflicting messages and broken promises; a merry-go-round of break-ups and reconciliations; and buckets of tears. Dave was struggling within himself and I was struggling to hang on to "what could be" and together we were toxic.

It was a 12-month detour in the prime of my life; a hard lesson, but I came away the wiser. My Nikes now reside prominently by the front door and I'm not afraid to use them—just test me! ▉

Couch
Stud
(I Mean
"Dud")

B ryan was a professional basketball player. At 7-feet 2-inches tall and 315 pounds his mere presence would silence a room. At 5-feet 5-inches tall, I was a midget next to him. As looks go, he was surprisingly easy on the eyes.

My first date with Bryan proved to be a comfortable evening of conversation and laughs. That is, once we found a table where he could sit without raising it off the floor with his knees. Bryan recited a list of morals and traditional family values that would win over the most protective parents. He painted a clear picture of the life he was seeking—a loving woman whom he would cherish and forever place on a pedestal; a brood of happy children; and a home in the country, custom designed for a giant, but considerate of "her" wishes, as well. It was a good story and it seemed sincere. At the end of our date, Bryan walked me to my car where he presented me with a single red rose, thanked me for a wonderful evening, and kissed me softly on the cheek. When I arrived home there was a message on the answering machine from Bryan telling me again what a great time he had had and wishing me sweet dreams.

The following day a beautiful flower arrangement was delivered to my office. The card read "From Your Biggest Fan" and then proceeded with a request for a second date. I was smitten to say the least.

For our second date Bryan, who lived 65 miles away, suggested driving up during the week, meeting me at my office, and taking me to lunch. I liked the idea because this way I could introduce him to some of my coworkers and garner their impressions albeit brief. The more opinions the better was my feeling.

The morning of our date I woke up to discover the ground had been blanketed overnight with about six-inches of snow. With the inclement weather I fully expected to receive a cancellation call. Bryan, sensing my surprise when he arrived, explained that nothing could have kept him away. Then he began to recite the familiar U.S. Postal motto: Neither snow nor rain nor heat nor gloom of night…

Lunch progressed as our first date had—easy, interesting, and fun. As we prepared to leave the restaurant I looked out the window and sighed. Bryan asked what was wrong. I explained I hadn't had time to clear my driveway or sidewalk before leaving for work and wasn't particularly looking forward to facing the task when I got home. Back at work, I thanked him for lunch, wished him a safe drive home, and we kissed. A very sweet, simple kiss. I floated all the way to my desk and remained airborne the rest of the day. Oh, the coworker consensus? Two thumbs up!

The rest of the afternoon flew by and at 5:30 p.m. I was headed home. During the 40-minute commute I tried not to dwell on the snow waiting to be cleared on such a bitter cold evening. I couldn't help but think how great it would be to skip the shoveling and just slip into my p.j.'s, sit in front of the fireplace, and enjoy a cup of hot peppermint tea. But, alas, I knew what had to be done and I heaved a big sigh as I turned the car onto my street.

My house was usually easy to spot after a snow because I was typically the last on my block to clear my walks. Everyone else was married with children (read "in-house human snowblowers"). But this night my house wasn't jumping out like normal; I did a double take. My driveway was completely cleared and the walks, too. I couldn't believe it. Are there such things as snow removal fairies? Well, whatever, the case, I pulled the car into the garage with a huge smile on my face. I could smell the tea brewing!

I dropped my briefcase in the foyer and went back out to get the mail. And that's when my smile got even bigger. In the mailbox was a long-stemmed white rose and a note from Bryan which read:

Put your legs up, relax, and have a nice evening.
Fondly,
Bryan

Bryan definitely scored big with this—it was such a simple gesture, but it meant so much. Bryan, it seemed, was a real catch.

I slipped into my p.j.'s, started a fire, got the tea ready, and telephoned Bryan.

"Bryan, it's Victoria. I just got home and I can't believe what you did; very sweet! I was whining all the way home about having to deal with the snow and so it was a great surprise. Thanks so much!"

"I'm glad. Lunch was nice today and I didn't want you to have to "work" tonight."

"When will I see you again?"

"The team is on a road trip starting Thursday, I come home Tuesday. Can I call you then?"

"Absolutely. I look forward to it."

"Sweet dreams."

"You too."

I took a sip of my hot peppermint tea and did, in fact, enjoy sweet dreams.

As promised, Bryan telephoned the following Tuesday. "Where are you calling from?" I asked.

"I'm on the airplane; we're getting ready to leave Boston. We should land around 7 p.m. Can I interest you in a late dinner?"

No arm twisting required here, "That would be nice" I replied.

"Let me tell you what sounds good to me, Victoria, and then tell me what you think. I'd like to go to an upscale, elegant restaurant. Somewhere we won't be bothered or rushed; somewhere quiet. How does that sound?"

"Exactly right."

"Since we are getting ready to take-off, would you mind making the reservation? Let's say 9 p.m. to be safe. Be sure to use my name—that will help."

"Not a problem; I'll handle it."

"I can't wait to see you."

"Bye."

And so it was a 9 p.m. reservation at the city's most chic restaurant. They assured me we would be seated at the best table in the house and attentively serviced until we were ready to go. Who says "a name" doesn't make a difference?

At approximately 7:30 p.m. Bryan telephoned from the car to say he was about 15 minutes away from my house. He wanted to make sure everything was set and to ask if he could use my guest room to change for dinner. No problem. Bryan looked very debonair in his navy suit and bright-colored tie. I wore a simple black cocktail dress.

As we were shown to our table, heads turned and there was a buzz as fellow patrons recognized my dinner companion. Thankfully, we were seated in a private cove so we could enjoy conversation without intrusion. Bryan ordered a nice bottle of merlot (my favorite) and the evening was underway. He brought me up-to-date on his team's winning road trip, including the fact that he had had an all-time personal best for points scored in a game. We talked about horses. Once he retired from basketball it was his dream to live on a huge spread in the country and raise Clydesdales. We talked about what I was looking for in a relationship. Someone who was willing to take things slow and form a friendship first. So many of the guys I had gone out with acted as though dating was a race for sex; their focus was more about how quickly they could get you in bed than it was about anything else. Date 1— take her out and give her a good-night kiss. Date 2— take her out and feel her up. Date 3—take her out and take her to bed. I cannot tell you how many guys stopped calling me once they figured out I was not willing to play by this clock.

We talked about what we were looking for in a relationship. Bryan said he, too, wanted to solidify a friendship first, and then he talked more about his traditional upbringing and how important that had been in shaping his life. It was so refreshing! We talked about the places he had traveled, endorsements he had done, and movies he had appeared in—as an extra.

The latter particularly intrigued me as I had been in a few movies myself, also as an extra. Turns out, Bryan was in a brief scene in my all-time favorite Christmas movie. "Are you kidding me?" I asked "I absolutely love that movie. I watch it every year; it's tradition. In fact, I own the videotape. What scene are you in?" Now there was urgency to finish dinner and go home to watch the video.

Poor, Bryan. The guy had just flown across the country and all he wanted to do was sit and enjoy a relaxing meal, but now he had to hurry and finish his dinner so this gal, whom he had had all of three dates with, could go home and see where he was in this silly movie. Bryan very good-naturedly honored my request.

As I unlocked the front door, I said to Bryan:

"I need to check my answering machine to see if my morning appointment has confirmed. Go ahead into the living room…you'll find the videotapes in the cabinet; I'll only be a minute."

I walked down the hall to my study. There was a message waiting—my 8 o'clock meeting was on. I hit the "save" button and headed back to the living room—'show time,' I thought to myself, 'this should be fun.' As I came around the corner I got a show all right, but not the kind I had invited, expected, or wanted. There—stretched out across my white Italian leather sectional—was Bryan in all his butt-naked glory. So disrespectful! I was outraged and appalled! Without a nanosecond of hesitation, I yelled out in drill sergeant like fashion:

"You have exactly 60 seconds to put your clothes back on and get out of my house! I can't believe you would disrespect me like this in my own home!"

I could feel the anger raging through me like a wild fire. So much for traditional values and all the other lines he used on me. Bryan looked up with an exaggerated pout on his face. This made things even worse from my perspective, which, of course, was the only perspective that mattered at this point. I picked his pants up off the floor and threw them at him.

"If you don't get out of here right now, I'm calling the police...MOVE!"

Completely unaffected, Bryan pointed to a wrapped package setting on the coffee table and said, "I got you something. Open it. I think it's the right size."

"I'm not interested in presents; I want you to leave."

Still indifferent, Bryan calmly opened the package and held up the contents—a skimpy, whore red negligee. "Here," he said, standing up and walking toward me, "try it on. Let's see how it looks; let's see how it does."

I immediately stepped back, picked up the phone, and started counting...60...59...58...57... At this, Bryan became furious.

"Do you know who you're talking to? I'm a star; girls throw themselves at me. Any one of a hundred girls would kill to have this opportunity right now. I make more money in one year than you will in a lifetime. I get what I want and I'm not leaving until I do."

"You can either get dressed and leave on your own; or you can leave in handcuffs in the back of a police car. Your choice. 56...55...54..."

All my senses were on high alert. I looked Bryan square in the eyes, stood my ground, and kept counting down. He gathered his clothes. When I got to 21 seconds, Bryan was dressed and on his way out of the house.

"You're going to be sorry, Victoria; no girl talks to me like this. You don't know who you're dealing with."

"One, I'm not a girl. Two, I never want to hear from or see you again…ever."

The tone of my voice and deathly stare provided the appropriate exclamation point, and, with that, I slammed the door behind him and watched through the window to make sure he drove away. Once his car was out of sight the seriousness of the situation hit me and I began to shake; then cry.

After some good cleansing sobs, I retreated to the bedroom and called my friend, Diana—it was 12:40 a.m. Diana offered a sympathetic ear and her typical level-headed advice (yes, she was logical even at that ridiculous hour). We spoke for about 20-minutes, just enough to calm me down and bring some levity to the situation. I hung up thinking that perhaps I would be able to sleep after all. Then the phone rang.

"Hello?"

"Yeah, Victoria, it's Bryan. Listen, I just got pulled over by the State Patrol. I need you to talk to the officer. He pulled me over for speeding and reckless driving. I think if you tell him about our fight he'll let me go."

Oh, of *course,* the officer will let you go; everyone knows that fighting with your "girlfriend" is an excuse which supersedes any traffic law violation—moron! I was getting ready to hang up when I heard a voice in the background sternly order:

"Sir, hang up the phone! Sir, hang up the phone—now!"

Bryan replied:

"My girlfriend is on the phone; she wants to talk to you...she can explain."

There was a moment of static and the line went dead. Okay, a weird evening had just become more so. Emotionally drained, I fell asleep.

The phone rang again—it was 2:39 a.m. Startled and still half asleep, I groggily answered:

"Hello?"

"Victoria, it's Bryan. Don't hang up! They arrested me and I'm in jail. You're my one phone call. They impounded my car and everything. I need you to come down and bail me out."

Bad call, Bryan! I mean if you are only allowed one call, I certainly would not recommend ringing anyone who said she "never wanted to see or hear from you again...ever." Without uttering a word, I unplugged the phone and went back to sleep.

Two years later, and obviously still grappling with the concept that some women actually say what they mean and mean what they say, "Couch Dud" left the following message on my answering machine:

"Victoria, it's Bryan...you remember. I'm taking the trooper to court and I really need you as a witness. The case is set for next Tuesday at 10:30 a.m. I'm counting on you to be there."

Tempting offer, but unfortunately that was the same day I was scheduled to clean behind the refrigerator—Bryan was going to have to count me out. ▨

My Family is Crazy, But I'm Normal

Bob was a special guy. Special in the sort of way that a room in which the walls, floor, and ceiling are padded is special. Got the picture? Good. Now caution: you're about to enter Bob's world.

Bob and I met through work. He was one of three consultants assigned to get our accounting department on-line with a new computer system and I was the person assigned to keep track of the consultants. In other words, I was a well-paid babysitter. Bob was a great listener, and, being a very young bachelor, had all the old married women in the department wanting to mother him. By the time the project wrapped, Bob had not only won over a team of adopted moms, but he had also piqued my interest. Shortly thereafter, we began dating and things moved along fairly well…until…let's just say that my intuition was telling me that not all the pieces were in the puzzle box.

Bob and I were seeing each other about two days a week (and more when we could). He spoke frequently of his best friend, Jeff, (someone he had known since the fifth grade) and his family (his parents, one older brother, and two younger sisters) all of whom lived in town. So, after several months of dating it was curious to me that our paths had not crossed—if not by plan, by chance—the community wasn't that big. Bob had shown me pictures of his family and I knew what each of them did for a living and what recreational pursuits they enjoyed. But meet them? Nope, not today, not tomorrow, and not—it seemed—in the near future. It wasn't long before the invisible friend and family thing created a wall of secrecy and was negatively impacting our relationship. Also, I was beginning to notice that some of Bob's stories didn't add up. Things like he claimed to be debt-free and I knew he made good money, but he was almost always short on cash. He claimed to have a bulging savings account, but the balance shown on a recent statement clearly indicated otherwise. He drove a 12-year-old car (no, it wasn't a "classic") and his apartment was sparse to put it kindly. Before anyone jumps to the wrong conclusion here, I have no problem—absolutely none—with frugal living. What I do have a problem with is when two plus two doesn't equal four.

It was time to do some investigative work. I gave Bob an ultimatum—lunch for four (his parents and us) or lunch for one (Bob without me—permanently). I did not understand what the big deal was and Bob's excuses were weak at best. Good grief, I wasn't asking for a "meet the parents I'm going to marry her" lunch—just a simple "hey, I really do have parents" lunch would do nicely, thank you. So lunch for four it was—Bob and I with Kevin and Barbara—at a restaurant about 40 miles outside of town. Never in my wildest dreams would I have imagined that I was about to meet the "Planter family" (think "nuts").

My initial impression of Kevin and Barbara was they were stiff, robotic, cold, and very unhappy human beings. I was beginning to see Bob's hesitation, but my battle scar motto was "out of the gate; get it straight." In other words, get to the root of the truth as soon as possible—whatever the truth is.

So, here we were—the four of us—nibbling away at the appetizer and trying mightily to keep the conversation rolling when, out of nowhere, Bob's mom went psycho. And I do mean this in the

mentally insane sense. Her voice changed, her facial
expressions became monster scary, and she was
yelling at the top of her lungs—at me! I sat straight
up in my chair in absolute shock and amazement.
She was screaming, "Get her out of here. Get the
bitch out of here." And, just in case any of the
dining patrons missed those elegant words, she
repeated it three more times before Bob, his father,
and several of the wait staff were able to restrain her
and move her to a secluded area.

Speechless, bewildered, and with jaw in the full
dropped position, I sat there. What in the heck was
that about? Our waiter asked if I was okay and if he
could get me anything. Yeah, how about a straight-
jacket for her and a taxi for me.

After a good while, Bob returned to the table.

"Everything is okay now; she thought you were
a witch."

"A witch?"

"Yes, but she's okay now. She must have
forgotten to take her medication this morning. Dad
has her in the car; we need to go."

"What do you mean she thought I was a witch? What happened here, Bob?"

"It's a long story. Let's just say this afternoon you met one of my mother's personalities; she has a few."

Back in the car, everything was back to "normal" and the first puzzle was solved—I now understood why Bob had selected an out-of-the-way restaurant. And, for you "inquiring minds," Barbara had five personalities—I met two.

Soon there were so many skeletons flying out of the closet that I felt as if I were in some bizarre Halloween flick. Barbara tried to stab Bob with a knife. Bob confessed to setting fire to his parents' house. Kevin was fired from yet another job. Barbara made threatening calls to her sister and was temporarily placed in a mental facility.

It was time to bid adieu to Bob and the rest of the "Planter family" and I did so with restraining order in hand, never looking back. (Nut) Case closed! ☒

Going the Distance (Long Distance)

I met Steve while dining alone one Friday night at a popular downtown restaurant. I had been immersed in the pile of reading material that I had brought along to keep me entertained when he approached my table. He looked ridiculously young to my eyes; easily five to six years younger than me I surmised. He was strikingly handsome with perfectly styled dark chocolate hair and complementing eyes. He was only slightly taller than I with a build to indicate he was no stranger to the gym. A nice picture, indeed!

Steve asked if he could join me, quickly explaining that he, too, was dining alone. Unbeknownst to me, he had been seated at the bar waiting for his table when he caught sight of me. He said he thought I was very cute and was drawn to my ponytail hairstyle. The next thing I knew the waitstaff was sweeping up; the restaurant had been officially closed for over an hour. During dinner I had learned that Steve actually resided in Indiana and was only in town for the weekend to attend an important football game of his alma mater. He was a die-hard college football fan. I also learned that Steve was actually only one year and 20 days younger than me. Further, he had broken off an engagement eight months earlier after learning his fiancée had been unfaithful. We connected in a way that felt as if we had known each other forever. We exchanged business cards and Steve invited me to join him for dinner the following evening for an "official" first date. I did not hesitate—yes, of course I would!

As Steve escorted me to my car he said, "I want you to know that tonight you single-handedly revived my faith that there are still quality single women left in this world." I blushed.

We met at 7 p.m. same restaurant, same table, and, for the second night in a row, we left with the janitorial staff. It was a wonderful evening. I was amazed at how comfortable and at ease I was with this man. We had remarkably similar backgrounds, values, interests, and goals. He was genuinely funny with a refreshingly optimistic view on life. His favorite quote was "Don't sweat the small stuff and it's all small stuff."

Out in the parking lot we sat on the curb and gazed at the moon. "You know" he said "I thought I was only coming to Colorado to catch a football game, but I think I may have caught my wife." I have no idea what kind of odd contortions my face went into at that precise moment, but the words, albeit surprising, felt comfortably right. We remained in the parking lot for a good hour, talking, dancing to the tunes from the car's CD player, and talking, talking, talking. It was obvious that neither of us wanted the night to end. Finally, realizing he only had five hours until his flight home, we parted with a series of passionate kisses.

For the next 11 months Steve and I spoke regularly via telephone. First it was once every couple of weeks, then weekly, then several times a week, then daily—and, ultimately, several times throughout the day.

Then one Saturday while on one end of the telephone line Steve was painting the baseboards in his house and I, on the other end, was doing laundry, Steve interrupted the dialogue and said, "I have something to say and I'm just going to say it. You don't need to say anything, but I want you to know that I have feelings for you—feelings of love—

Victoria, I love you." What wonderful words! I, too, was becoming very attached, but I had been reluctant to share the depth of my feelings for fear of being hurt should the affection not be mutual. With the words now spoken there was no denying that our long-distance relationship was a close friendship which showed clear signs of becoming a love relationship. It was the track we both wanted.

Steve and I continued to talk openly about key relationship issues such as religion, children, family, money, sex, etc. Our conversations solidified the match; the foundation was unquestionably there. We had reached the proverbial crossroads; this telephone relationship was no longer enough. We had to meet again to verify the connection and, if the connection was truly there (as we both expected), one of us would have to move.

Coincidentally, at this same time I was awarded with an all-expense-paid trip to Hawaii from my employer. Our meeting place was set—Maui, Hawaii. We spent the next six weeks planning. I sent him piles of catalogs and brochures—everything from hotels to golf courses to sunset cruises to restaurants—all for his input and vote. We were like kids the night before Christmas—the anticipation was barely controllable.

It was now two weeks before our trip and I was positively walking on air; no one could knock me off this cloud. Steve and I were talking three and four times a day. The sheer excitement of being together again (especially in Hawaii) was absolutely explosive! People were actually commenting about my "glow."

Monday came—six days and counting down. I had barely settled in at my desk when the phone rang. It was Steve and two seconds into the call I knew something was wrong. "Steve, I can tell in your voice that something isn't right. So, listen to me…I want you to speak slowly, clearly, and truthfully." After a brief pause he began…

"I found out a few weeks ago, through some friends, that my old college sweetheart recently got divorced. She has two kids, ages 6 and 10, and no money. Her husband got the house and she got custody of the children. I moved her into my house over the weekend. Our families have known each other for years and when I heard her marriage didn't work out...well, it just seemed like a sign. I know we have been making plans of our own and we have this trip to Hawaii in less than a week. I have told Carol about you and about our trip. She isn't particularly thrilled about me going with you because she and I have talked about possibly pursuing a future together. However, I just can't leave you in a bind. I didn't mean for this to happen; I don't want to hurt you. So, I guess what I'm saying is I'll still go with you to Maui."

I'm stunned, I'm speechless, and I'm at work. Way to go, Steve. The silence was too much for him so he started up again.

"Victoria, you're a great person; a rare gem. You truly are beautiful inside and out..."

Okay, stop already. I didn't need to be flattered or stroked. Did he really think his words held any meaning at this point? Trying hard to compose myself and maintain a calm, steady voice I responded:

"Steve, I am going to say a few words and then I am going to hang up. I don't expect you to interrupt. First, consider yourself officially uninvited to Hawaii and save the flowery fluff for Carol. It was cowardly and terribly inconsiderate of you to telephone me at work with this news. I can't even begin to put my feelings into words. Second, I believe you are making a very big mistake, but it is your mistake to make. Just be clear that should your plans not work out next week, next month, next year, or a decade from now, don't call me. Don't ever call me again."

With that said I slammed the phone into its cradle.

Six months later (in fact, on my birthday) Steve called. His relationship with his college sweetheart had not worked out. Now *there* was a news flash. Was I seeing anyone? "No," and that especially included anyone named Steve. Aloha, baby!

(For the record, I did go to Hawaii—guy free—and had a fabulous time...thanks for asking.) X

Are You
Impressed
Yet?

Just thinking about my *one* date with Scotty O. is enough to make my skin crawl. The only thing this guy needed sitting across the table was a mirror.

Let's start with his name, shall we? He told me the "O" stood for "opulence." I think "odd" or "oaf" would have been more on the mark, but that's just my opinion. Scott was his middle name; he preferred Scotty—it was more "snappy." Of course, there is nothing wrong with "snappy" I just wonder at what age you don't need to be so...Scotty O. was 51.

Scotty boy was in real estate—The Donald Trump of Denver to hear him tell the tale. Any office building in the city was a deal hustled, negotiated, and closed by him. Yes, he was the ultimate one-man show (I suspect in more ways than one). But there's more... It was pretty obvious that Scotty O. had had some encounter with the elusive fountain of youth. Allow me to paint the picture—51-year-old male, mid-life crisis in full swing, platinum card screaming to be swiped, and the magical work of a plastic surgeon who got hold of this swinger and his credit card. It was a face lift that subliminally made me think about saran wrap—ummm, wonder if I need to add that to my grocery list? I'm not knocking the look; after all, it held the potential for a great deal of entertainment value. Think about it…knock down a few cocktails and—boom—you're making conversation with a puppet.

A face of plastic and a personality to match; what more could a woman hope for? The night was all about Scotty O.—he absolutely said so. The heart-melting words were uttered about 45 minutes into the date when he finally came up for air…

"So you see, Victoria, I'm really quite the catch. I know what I want and I have the means to get it. Really, it's all about me at this point."

"Fascinating…" was the only word I could come up with, spoken in the same tone I might use if I had just spent weeks watching grass grow. "Snappy" didn't miss a beat, he dove right back into his self-absorbed monologue. At about the 60-minute mark, his jabbering became just a slightly annoying buzz in my ears…blah, blah, blah, blah, blah… I was actually impressed to have held off the "glazed eyes" look this long—log this date into the record books, boys and girls!

It was time for an exit strategy. Over an hour together and the only question he had asked me was what did I want to drink. Correction, that was the waiter's question. Silly me. It truly was all about Scotty O. He had made me a believer...the only thing he needed to get along happily in life was a mirror and an oxygen tank.

My mind was overflowing with questions for "Snappy:"

1. Where is your "mute button" and would you mind testing it?
2. Do you ever worry about lock jaw?
3. How long can you hold your breath? Please demonstrate.
4. Have you ever met anyone more interesting than yourself? Fascinating...

So many questions, but, alas, my desire to break away from his droning took precedence over further entertainment value. It was time to call it a night.

To do so, I knew I would have to be aggressive; otherwise he might not notice I was gone. On second thought, would that be so bad? I stood up. Scotty O.

continued on for a few more sentences and then asked, "Are you going somewhere?"

"Yes, I'm going home."

"Okay."

It was all very matter-of-fact, and, suffice it to say, strange. We walked out to the parking lot. His Porsche was in the south lot; my Subaru was in the north lot. I extended my hand and wished him a good evening.

"If you ever want to get together again, Victoria, give me a call. Here's my card."

Safely in my car, I wrote on the back of "Snappy's" business card, "Next date: When pigs fly."

Boys and girls, a round of applause please, for the one, the only Scotty O. ▧

Now You
See Him;
Now You
Don't

Phil was a surgeon, 45, divorced 13 years, childless, and a typical commitment phobic, among other things. He split his time between his medical practice in Santa Barbara, California, and Vail, Colorado. We met by coincidence at a holiday party and exchanged business cards.

About two weeks later Phil telephoned. This is when I learned that not only did I have this uncanny ability to attract every loser, creep, jerk, and weirdo in my state, but my skill seemed to work equally well across state lines.

Phil and I had not communicated since our initial introduction over the holidays, so when the telephone rang and it was Phil I was expecting to ease into conversation that would pick up where we had left off. That was my mindset when Phil, right after he said hello, hit me with, "Do you have a No. 2 pencil? I'm going to give you a test." Yes—you heard right—a test; it was a bad flashback to when the teacher would announce "pop quiz!"

For the next 60 minutes (give or take) Phil administered the Myers-Briggs personality test to me...all 70 questions. Then he scored it. My Myers-

Briggs Type Indicator (MBTI) was identified as EFSJ. I don't remember what being an EFSJ supposedly suggested about my personality, but I do remember that his MBTI was not a strong complement to mine. And I'll never forget that we spent another hour talking about our MBTI differences (well, Phil talked; I mostly listened). It would not be a stretch to say that Phil was borderline obsessive about the all-revealing, all-predicting Myers-Briggs. He was a Myers-Briggs believer. Can I hear an "Amen!" boys and girls?

Suffice it to say, we were off to an unusual start, but I was cautious not to lose objectivity. For one, I liked Phil's sarcastic sense of humor. Two, he was an interesting intellect. Three, he showed some caring traits. Add these three things up and his quirkiness was small potatoes.

Phil's career and two-state office arrangement meant that 90 percent of our "dating" was of the phone variety, and, first phone date aside, we had some very riveting conversations. You cannot learn everything there is to know about a person over phone lines, but you can make a pretty good dent.

Phil had provided me with every number imaginable so I could reach him anywhere, anytime—his private office line, his cellular, his pager, his home telephone, his e-mail, and his assistant was under strict orders to find him whenever I called. So, although Phil wasn't physically available, he was about as technologically available as one could be. We spoke at least three to four times a week for several months, and then—poof!—he was gone.

What do I mean by "gone?" If you want to label his disappearance, please select from the following:

❏ Cold feet
❏ Relationship suffocation
❏ Too comfortable, too fast.

Years earlier, I would have spent an inordinate amount of time analyzing the situation and placing blame on myself for him pulling back. Thank goodness I wised up! I placed a single phone call to his home to say I had enjoyed getting to know him and wished him well. Then I simply "let it go." That, ladies, is freedom.

It was early June when I next heard from Phil. He blamed his absence on a busier than normal workload (just to be clear, I didn't ask for an explanation) and soon we were back into our previous pattern. By August, you guessed it, he was gone again.

This cycle continued for two more runs, in total just over a year, before I completely tired of the merry-go-round.

"Phil, are you interested in marrying again, honestly?"

"Some days I think I want to, but other days I'm really glad to be alone. To be completely honest, I'm not comfortable with the "C" word. My first marriage was difficult; we fought all the time. I think you are a fine woman, Victoria, but I worry because as an ESFJ we clash in some critical areas. I swear by the accuracy of the Myers-Briggs test; we have used it as part of the employment screening in my medical practice for years and it has yet to throw us a curve."

"Wow, I failed my first test at 37, imagine that."

"If it helps, you're in good company—no one I have dated the past dozen years has been a strong complement to my score. Why can't we just continue 'as is.' Perhaps with a little more time…"

"'As is?' I don't think so."
Caveat emptor, sister! ▉

Mirror,
Mirror,
Magical
Mirror

Dennis was another one of those "fix-up dates." My parents first met on a blind date and four decades later are still so much in love it's just downright sappy. I, on the other hand, was not having a morsel of success with this format. In fact, the whole fix-up thing was becoming rather annoying. Let's see, stay home and tweeze my eyebrows or go meet Mr. Possibility. I've got to tell you, there were plenty of times when the tweezing thing was clearly the smarter option. Any who… history was teaching me that a few introductory telephone calls as a prelude to a fix-up could sometimes be a good predictor of the face-to-face event.

Dennis described himself as a young 48-year-old, well-traveled, Ivy League graduate, and owner of a successful business. "I consider myself very handsome" he said without a hint of arrogance. "I'm tall, fit, and have great hair." It is important to note that it has always been my nature to take people at their word—I never developed a suspicious/distrustful mind…or at least I didn't before my date with Dennis. Lesson to be learned: Skepticism can be a good thing.

We agreed to meet at 8 p.m. Thursday at a wine bar downtown. A light snow was just starting to fall when I arrived at the bar about a quarter past eight. No Dennis. I stood patiently near the entrance for about 15 minutes and then impatiently paced the floor near the entrance for another 10 minutes. Just as I was getting ready to label myself "officially stood up," in walks a lone gentleman. This *had* to be Dennis, I thought. But, wait…as he started to take off his wraps it was clear he didn't fit Dennis' description—at all. For starters, this guy was bald and Dennis had said he had "great hair."

"Victoria?"

"Dennis?"

Oh, my gosh, it was Dennis! What kind of magical mirror did this guy employ? Let's separate fact from delusion, shall we?

Dennis' Magical Mirror (DMM): Young 48-year-old.

Harsh Reality (HR): Since Dennis actually looked much older than his age, I had to hope this descriptor was not a reference to his age in dog years.

DMM: Very handsome.

HR: Let's go with "average" and leave it at that.

DMM: Tall.

HR: Bing, bing—he got one right, he was tall.

DMM: Fit.

HR: Having a pronounced pot belly doesn't equate to "fit" in my book. What bothered me most about this descriptor was that if the shoe were on the other foot…well, let's just say the magnification we women folk are under from you male folk is often unforgiving, even ruthless. Time to suck it up, buckaroos—there's Weight Watchers or there's lipo.

DMM: Great hair.

HR: It had to be on his chest or back because I'm telling you it wasn't on his head.

We located a quiet spot and began to peruse the menu. Well, actually, Dennis perused the menu; I tried to quiet the noise in my head—something about not judging this first impression too harshly. But it wasn't working—for two reasons. No. 1, and very importantly, since the physical description Dennis gave me over the phone was so far from reality, I wanted to know why he chose to be misleading. I mean, I wasn't expecting to have drinks with Mr. Clean's twin brother. And, No. 2, either way I did not find him physically attractive.

The waiter approached our table:

"Good evening and welcome to The Grape Vine. My name is Brett and I will be your server this evening. I must say, it's so great to see a father and daughter spending time together—very nice. What can I bring for you?…Miss?"

Directions to the back door works for me, thank you. Okay, the rough start just got rougher…now Mr. Clean was my dad…ugh! To his credit, Dennis let the comment go without injury to the waiter, and, boom, we had an instant conversation starter.

We kept residence at the bar for almost two hours. The dialogue was pleasant enough, but, honestly, I think the father-daughter image (forget the Mr. Clean look-alike) did this pairing in at the clinking of the glasses.

Cheers! X

Full
Moon

This was the evening of my long-awaited date with Tony, a guy I had been pining over for months. He was handsome, smart, and successful. He was funny, well-traveled, and interesting. And this evening he was my date.

I about fell over when I received his telephone call asking me to dinner. Could it be? Really? Me? Finally! Tony had dated a lot. I had caught glimpses of a few of his girlfriends and had heard stories about others. Most of his "selections" didn't seem to fit; granted, my feelings were swayed by my own desire for this man and opinion that I was absolutely the perfect woman for him. As soon as I hung up the phone, I began to plan my outfit, hair, jewelry, makeup, the whole ball of wax. I was so excited!

The afternoon of our date, I had an appointment with a celebrated stylist; the owner of the city's most elite salon. She knew about my big date and soon the whole salon was in on it. When it was all over, my nails, makeup, and hair were absolutely perfect. My hair looked very "Grace Kelly" in the most glamorous "up do" ever. Walking to my car, a gentleman passerby said I looked "stunning." That did it, I was radiating. Bring on Tony!

Pick up time was set for 7 p.m., but it seemed Tony wanted to test the "fashionably late" rule, landing on my porch just before half past the hour. His tardiness started the dominoes falling as we raced at a fire drill pace to answer the all-important question: Can we make that 7:45 p.m. dinner reservation? Okay, so we weren't going to ease into the evening, I was just happy to have the date underway.

Once seated, I took one look into those big green eyes and melted. I swear Tony could wear a plastic garbage bag and still look good. He had gorgeous sun-kissed hair, a body-builder physique, and was a commanding presence at 6-feet 4-inches tall. More importantly, he had a pleasing sense of humor and a good disposition. Unfortunately, it seemed I caught him on an off night...

"You look very handsome tonight, Tony."

"Thanks."

Alrighty then...no compliments were coming back over the net. I had spent all afternoon at the salon primping for this date and if I had to say so myself (and all indications were leaning that direction) I was looking pretty fine. And this hair, how could he not comment on the hair? Come on, a complete stranger noticed!

The conversation was stimulating and time flew by. Unlike any other first date I had ever had we hit all the "taboo subjects" right out of the gate—politics, religion, financial ideologies, sex. It was refreshing and bold, just like Tony. I was having a delightful time and all signals seemed to indicate that the feeling was mutual. So what could possibly go wrong you ask; well, brace yourself.

The restaurant bordered a park so after dinner Tony proposed a walk before taking me home. The night air was warm and the sky was brightly lit thanks to a full moon—spectacular. As we walked hand-in-hand I wondered if this was the moment Tony would shower me with compliments. Okay, maybe "shower" was too much to ask; I would have settled for a raindrop. As we reached the lake, Tony turned, looked straight into my eyes, and said, "Your hair needs work."

Okay, is there a doctor around here because obviously there is something terribly wrong with my hearing.

"Excuse me?"

"Your hair…it looks awful and…and, well, it stinks."

"Stinks? Are you kidding me? You mean stinks like a skunk or what exactly?"

"No, not as bad as that…it just smells…I don't know…bad."

I probably looked like a deer in the headlights at this point. I just couldn't believe this was happening. I mean, what do you say to something like that?

"Tony, I'm not exactly sure what to say. I just spent four hours at the most elite salon in this city getting ready for our date. I'm not sure what it is your nose is sensing, but I can assure you there are no strange, offensive, or foul odors coming from my hair or anywhere else on my body. Frankly, I find it bizarre to even be talking about this and am hurt that the only comment you could think to make this entire evening about my appearance was that my hair looks awful and smells bad."

"It's just the thing that stands out and I'm an honest guy. I don't think that hairstyle is the best look for your face and your hair does, in fact, smell. Maybe it's a fragrance in the shampoo that doesn't agree with your body chemistry."

"Gosh, I didn't realize you were a hairstylist in a previous life? Or a chemist?"

"Now that wasn't nice."

"Nice? You're going to lecture me about nice?"

And you can probably guess how it went from there... Where is Vidal Sassoon when you need him? Or, for that matter, a bloodhound. Scratch the latter, I had dinner with him.

Chalk one up to the weirdness that can only happen on the night of a full moon. ⊠

I Rest
My Case

A good friend once told me, "Victoria, I'm going to share with you the key to a happy life. Advice that, if you follow, will save you untold sleepless nights, gray hair, and stomach-eating ulcers. Never, never, never, NEVER marry a lawyer. In fact, don't even risk it—don't date one." And, boys and girls, I have to tell you, that was damn good advice—too bad I didn't follow it 100 percent. I dated a lawyer.

Jerry was 46 years old and fit perfectly the stereotypical profile of a hard-hitting, big city lawyer. Think Michael Douglas in Wall Street, but instead of a financier, picture an attorney. Perfectly coiffured, perfectly educated, perfectly presented.

Going into this date, I was actually quite optimistic. We had several mutual friends and they were all certain Jerry and I would hit it off. Based upon my blind date track record, I should have been void of all optimism, but this time seemed different. Still, it took a few months of coaxing by our friends to get Jerry and I to agree to meet, but we finally did succumb.

The setup was even good—a round of golf— Jerry, a couple we both knew, and me. I've heard it said that if you really want to learn about someone, golf with them. True or false? I was about to find out.

The plan was to be at Jerry's house by 9 a.m. As I pulled up, Sue was standing outside waiting for me.

"Good morning, Victoria! Are you nervous or excited?"

"Both."

"Come on in...Jerry is anxious to meet you."

I had just stepped foot into the doorway when "woof, woof, woof," Super Dog came bouncing toward me at full speed, jumped up, and proceeded to bathe me in dog kisses. "Dallas" was a golden retriever weighing in somewhere in the neighborhood of 70 lbs. The dog, obviously friendly and good natured, had to be pulled off me. Now, I like dogs, but I wasn't particularly thrilled with starting my day (let alone a first date) with the remnant smell of dog slobber.

"Hello, Victoria, I'm Jerry. Nice to finally meet you. I see you've met Dallas."

"Yes, indeed; very friendly dog."

"She's my buddy. Let me show you around and then we'll get going."

Jerry's house was a lovely, simply appointed two-story home with wonderful golf course and mountain views from most every window, and it literally backed onto the fifth fairway.

"So how many windows have you had to replace due to wayward golf shots?"

"Unfortunately, more than one would think. The funny thing is I paid a premium for this lot, but, in retrospect, the developer should have paid me to take it."

Ah, a good temperament. The house was bright, airy, neat, and livable—he definitely had a housekeeper.

After the house tour we piled into Jerry's Land Rover and drove the five minutes to the golf club.

Jerry and Ed went to check us in as Sue and I proceeded to the practice range.

"So, Victoria, what do you think?"

"It's early, but so far so good."

"Well, he likes what he sees so far. Keep it up."

Keep it up? Whatever was that supposed to mean? We warmed up for about 30 minutes and then were called to the first tee. Sue and Ed in one cart; Jerry and I in the other—or at least that was the way it was supposed to be.

"Victoria, I'm going to walk. You take the cart."

Okey dokey, there went one opportunity to get to know more about Jerry for the next five hours. And so it went for the entire 18 holes. Jerry and Ed were pretty decent golfers; Sue and I weighed in on the beginner end. This meant that wherever Sue and I were on a hole, Jerry and Ed probably were not— trees, bunkers, water—and another opportunity was lost. By the end of the round, Sue and I were sufficiently caught up with each other's lives, but Jerry and I had barely exchanged a handful of words.

The good news was it had to get better from here. It was time for lunch and that setting would certainly give us a chance to get acquainted. But, how foolish of me, I failed to factor in the men's golf law whereby all shots in a round must be re-lived and, if necessary, analyzed. And so it went. The guys stepped through their replay and Sue and I continued with the girl talk. After lunch, Jerry invited all of us back to his place.

We had barely settled in the living room, when Sue announced she and Ed needed to go. It was Sunday and she had to be at work early Monday to prep for a meeting. Just as I was thinking "great, this is my chance to finally talk to this guy," Jerry chimed in:

"Yes, me too. In fact, I have some paperwork to attend to this evening. Victoria, thanks for coming. I'll walk you to your car."

I was zero for four on the day. It had been an odd date in so many ways. Heck, who am I kidding, what date? At my car, Jerry extended his hand, but only to give me his business card:

"Call me if you need anything."

Yeah, sure, how about the name and number of a guy who is actually ready to date. Case dismissed. ▧

Old
Geezer

Cecil was never a "date"—not ever in my mind. "Professional acquaintance"—yes. "Grandfatherly figure"—I thought so. "Dating material"—you've got to be kidding. "Old geezer"—bingo!

Cecil was 77 years old, a widower, short, stalky, bald, and—did I mention—incredibly wealthy. I do believe Anna Nicole Smith might have had him on her radar screen once upon a time.

I came to know of Cecil through my boss, Sam; they were old friends (no pun intended). We had talked numerous times on the telephone, but didn't meet until I had been on the job for well over a year. One day Cecil stopped by the office to surprise Sam with football tickets—it was his way of saying thank you for a favor. Cecil was waiting in the lobby to hand me the envelope. "Ever been to a professional football game?" he inquired. "Once, many, many years ago," I replied. "It was a Monday night game against Green Bay. It snowed so much the city was shutdown for two days. So now I just enjoy it on television—much less hassle and a whole lot warmer."

"You need to go to another game," Cecil stated matter-of-factly. "I'm going to courier tickets to your house tomorrow. You'll sit in my private box as my special guest. In fact, do you have family in town? Invite them along, too. Here…write down your home address and telephone number for me." Cecil was not going to take "no" for an answer.

"Okay, Cecil" I said as I scribbled the requested information on the back of his business card, "you win this time."

As promised, four tickets were delivered to my home the next evening. At about 8 p.m. my telephone rang.

"Hello, Victoria, it's Cecil. Did the tickets reach you okay, love?"

"Yes, thank you, Cecil."

"Did you notice the parking pass? That will allow you to park in the player's lot. I've arranged for you to be met at the gate and ushered to the Stadium Club for dinner prior to the game so you need to arrive at least 90 minutes before kick-off. Will your parents and brother be joining you?"

"Yes, they are looking forward to it."

"Fabulous! Now, I had another thought. I'm hosting a season kick-off party this Saturday. It's an event I host each year for the wives and girlfriends of the players and coaches. I want you to attend as my special guest. It's important that you meet the right people, Victoria, and this is a wonderful opportunity. I'll have an invitation sent to your office tomorrow. Dress nice now, sweetie, it's a fancy affair."

Turning into the stadium parking lot the scene was almost comical—well, comical when you're driving a 7-year-old Subaru station wagon and have to decide whether to park it next to a Mercedes, Lexus, Porsche, Jaguar, or BMW. A greeter was stationed at the entrance to check invitations. "Welcome, Victoria. Lunch seating is assigned— you're at Table 10." There were probably three dozen women already scattered about the room and a dozen or so ladies still waiting to be "screened" by the greeter. There was absolutely no sign of Cecil and, of course, I knew not a soul. Just being there was like some sort of out-of-body-experience. I found Table 10 and my place card. Good, I was the first to arrive…now I could check the names of those with whom I would be dining. If I wasn't already feeling a bit uneasy, this sealed it—to my immediate right would be the wife of the starting quarterback and to my immediate left would be the wife of the head coach. I was still staring at the place cards when a lady approached the table and yelled, "Sarah, we're over here." Lizbeth was married to a starting receiver; Sarah was dating one of the linebackers. I introduced myself, we engaged in several minutes of meaningless chit-chat, and one-by-one the ladies arrived and the table was filled.

Now, I'm not a wallflower and I can mingle with the best of them, but this was like being at a family reunion and discovering that you're the black sheep. Baaaa....

After 20 excruciating minutes of "table time," Julie, the wife of the team's famed quarterback, turned to me and asked, "Excuse me, I hate to be rude, but *who* are you?" I explained that I was Cecil's guest (who, by the way, was still MIA) and that Cecil was a long-time personal friend of my boss. It was all so dreadfully awkward. "Ohhhhh..." was the reply and the table conversation resumed. Where were their season tickets this year? Anne's husband had just been traded by the New York

Giants; had they gotten settled in yet? How was Patty's new housekeeper working out? What weeknight would the football wives' club be meeting this year?

I could hear the "fat lady" warming up her vocal chords and knew it was time to make my exit. Just as I was about to execute my escape, Cecil approached the table. "Good afternoon, lovely ladies," he greeted us with a wide smile. *Everyone* knew Cecil and they all seemed to be genuinely fond of him. "Has everyone met Victoria?" he asked. Heads nodded. "Good, good" he said and that was that. As quickly as he had appeared, he vanished.

Cecil placed several telephone calls to me following the party. Had I enjoyed meeting everyone? Was I looking forward to the season opener? Did I need anything?

I arrived at the stadium opening day with my parents and brother a full two hours before kick-off as Cecil had prescribed. The energy of the crowd was amazing. We were met at the gate, escorted to the Stadium Club where the buffet was already in full swing, and promptly seated with three couples all of whom worked for Cecil in various capacities. Two of the couples had never been to a professional sporting event of any kind and were absolutely giddy with anticipation. At *this* "family reunion" I was not a black sheep.

Cecil had been "working the room" for some time before he found his way over to our table. "So, Victoria, these must be your parents," Cecil stated as he extended his hand "wonderful to meet you both. And your brother, too. Welcome!" We talked briefly before Cecil ushered us to his box so as not to miss the pre-game festivities.

Cecil's box was located directly above the 50-yard line and it was P-L-U-S-H. Cecil introduced us to the other two guests in the box—the former mayor and the current mayor of our fair city. I had to pinch myself. At half-time Cecil took me around to meet other key community people. Again, *everyone* knew Cecil. I don't remember who won the game—I don't even really remember *watching* the game—all I remember is that it was a great day!

As we made our way to the exit, Cecil stood at the door bidding each guest a good night.

"Thanks so much, Cecil, that was a real treat!"

"This is only the tip of the iceberg for you, love. It's your year for pampering and surprises."

Okay, I'm not sure exactly what he meant by that, but it didn't matter—I was very happily exhausted. Cecil was just a nice, old man—like a grandfather, I surmised—who truly seemed to enjoy doing nice things for others.

Almost immediately after the season opener, and for about the next month, I received a steady stream of invitations from Cecil to various dinners and social events. His persistence was so determined that I soon became uneasy and suspicious. What *was* his motive? Certainly, he wasn't looking to *date* me...was he? I mean, good grief, I was 47 years his junior! Cecil's money may have been able to buy him a lot of things, but a date with me wasn't one of them. In fact, to my knowledge there's another name for that type of an arrangement. I continued to ponder his motive and decline his invites. Then, very late one evening the telephone rang:

"Hello, Victoria, it's Cecil. I sense that perhaps you're uncomfortable with me, that perhaps you're reading something that isn't there. Nevertheless, I don't want to be a source of discomfort to you so I won't be calling anymore."

I felt terrible. Here my gut had been sensing "old geezer" when maybe his intentions were innocent—just someone to share a night out with; nothing more, nothing less.

Several months passed and I couldn't stop thinking how I must have come across as ungrateful and snobbish. I telephoned Cecil at his office.

"Hey, Cecil, it's Victoria. I was just thinking about you and wondering what kind of trouble you've been stirring up. Would you like to meet for dinner sometime?"

"I'm so glad to hear from you. Yes, let's have dinner...tonight."

Tonight? I wasn't thinking tonight! I didn't have plans, but...

"Well, okay...sure."

"Can you be downtown in time to accommodate a 6 p.m. dinner reservation? My apartment is located only a few blocks from the restaurant. Plan to meet at my place, I'm on the 26th floor, and we'll drive together."

Hoping Cecil would be ready to go, I rang the bell. "Good evening, Victoria. Come on in. We have a few minutes before we need to leave. I'll show you around." Cecil did have an incredible view of the city. "Very nice," I said as he referenced various points of interest "What time is our reservation?"

"We'll leave in a minute; let me finish showing you around. You have to see the view from the bedroom."

Geezer alert; geezer alert! Hello, Earth to Cecil, this is NOT a date!

I stopped in the doorway while Cecil proudly proceeded to the middle of the room and declared "See, I've got the best view of anyone. Isn't this a great bedroom? And *that,* he said pointing to the far corner, "is my massage table."

The maitre d' greeted Cecil by name and instructed our waiter to seat us at "Mr. B's regular table." Cecil was recognized by several of the other patrons who waved to him as we were seated. My stomach was in knots. Nice guy or old geezer? Nice guy or old geezer? Okay, one way to find out—let's talk. I started the ball rolling by asking Cecil what he thought about the results of the recent election.

"That massage table in my bedroom...I had two sisters take care of my needs. They were wonderfully gentle; they had the softest touch. They would switch off days so I was assured of a daily rub. I need to be massaged daily, you know. They were very beautiful, young girls and I took very good care of them. One of them I put through college, you know. Then one day they just quit coming. I don't know what happened, but now I don't have anyone to rub me and I need someone."

Then he put his hand on my knee and asked, "Can you rub me, Victoria, real soft and gentle like this? I'll pay you very well; I'll take care of you financially, I promise. You'll never want for anything."

Case solved—definitely an old geezer and, yes, he thinks I'm his date or, even worse, his new massage therapist. Needless to say, at that moment I could think of a lot of things I could do with hot oil—a vat of it.

"Cecil," I said as I motioned for the check "have your secretary check the Yellow Pages; I think this is a job for a professional."

Calling Anna Nicole... X

Matchmaker, Matchmaker

I had voluntarily pulled out of the dating game after an especially lousy encounter with a suitor and was, for the first time in a long while, really enjoying myself. It was amazing how much brighter, happier, and easier things were when I wasn't focused on the absence of a man in my life.

Then, just when I got real comfortable, they sucked me back in. "They" were my well-meaning friends. It seems an article about matchmaking had recently run on the front page of the Business section. Voilá, the seed was planted. According to the matchmaker interviewed for the article, her method was nearly foolproof. Well, guess what, not fool-proof enough; it turned out there were still plenty out there.

Here was the deal. Bonnie limited her roster of bachelors and bachelorettes to a maximum of 125 each. This way, she reasoned, she could offer truly personal assistance. Applying for her service did not guarantee acceptance. First, there was a two-hour, one-on-one interview, then a background check, then another interview with a "select committee," and then, if you passed, collection of her fee—a whopping non-refundable $2,500 for 12 months of matching. Keep your wallet out—there's more—for every "match" (read: "date") agreed to, the bachelor and bachelorette each paid Bonnie an additional $100.

Matches worked like this—you would choose the age (or age range) of the person you wanted to date; desired hair color; eye color; height; weight; education (even as detailed as selecting a particular college); desire for children; religious preferences; profession; recreational interests; and on and on and on. Few stones were left unturned. Bonnie would then look for a match. She was clear to caution that because this was a true two-way match, it could take months before a client would receive a call. When a match was identified, Bonnie would place a call to both the bachelor and bachelorette, leaving a detailed description of each person and their background. Assuming both parties were interested, the $100 fee was collected from the clients and the respective names and telephone numbers released.

The fee was pricey and the element of surprise all but eliminated—modern romance. My friends encouraged me to ponder the upside. If Bonnie did her job the way she laid it out, in the long run I would be saving a lot of time and frustration. Even a "bad" date with this setup should have paled in comparison to my other misadventures. I finally caved and decided to try it for a year.

Four weeks after becoming a client, Bonnie called me with a match:

Gary, age 46, 5-feet 7-inches tall, never married, some college, accountant, big outdoorsman...blah, blah, blah...

Gong! I phoned Bonnie:

"Hello, Bonnie, it's Victoria. I got your message regarding Gary and I'm a bit...well...surprised. There's more than a few traits that don't match my requirements. I am willing to be flexible on some things, but I was very specific about not being an "outdoorsy" person. To propose a date with a guy whose passion is camping, fishing, and hiking...well, I'd like to know your thought process."

"Victoria, I understand your hesitation; but listen... After going through my inventory of profiles, I have not been able to identify what I would consider to be a strong match. This, mind you, is after a month of searching. There is one guy who I think might have good potential, but I currently have him set up with another one of my clients. Now, should that relationship not work out… In the meantime, Gary isn't bad and I think you would have a lovely time. Sleep on it and let me know tomorrow."

So now I'm being told that for my hard earned $2,500 I could have a date with a guy who "isn't bad." I could do that all day long on my own, thank you very much. Let's review…the point of employing a "professional" was to weed out, sift through, screen, and otherwise ensure that I didn't have to have a cup of java with Mr. Isn't Bad. I didn't care if it took six months for Bonnie to find a match, but I did expect a match; not a "hey, he's better than nothing." We were not off to a good start. I telephoned Bonnie within the half-hour with a "no thanks."

About three weeks later, I received another message from Bonnie.

"Victoria, it's Bonnie. Sweetie, I picked up a new client today and he's terrific. I think the two of you could be a really great match. His name is

David, he is 37, and an architect. He was divorced almost a year ago and has two children, ages 11 and 8. He plays softball, coaches on the side, and enjoys camping on the weekends."

Rewind. Yep, she said everything I thought she said. Bring out the gong.

"Hello, Bonnie, it's Victoria. I just listened to your message."

"Oh, good, I think you're really going to like this guy. I've already heard back from David about your bio; he can't wait to meet you. So…?"

"Bonnie, when was the last time you read through my list of requirements?"

"As a matter of fact just the other day. Why?"

"Really?!?! Then why is that you are suggesting a match with a man with two young children, who, once again, likes outdoorsy activities. My goodness, he hasn't even been divorced for a year. Are you kidding me with this or what?"

My blood pressure was rising rapidly at this point.

"Bonnie, I hired you because you assured me your service would be specific to my requirements.

As of now, you are 0 for 2. I know a match might take two, three, four months, or maybe more, and I'm okay with that. What I am not okay with is you calling me with profiles that represent the opposite of what I am looking for. Are the qualities and standards I marked so unreasonable?"

"No, not at all. It's more of a problem of fitting you into the profile."

"Me?"

"It's your education, Victoria. You didn't go to an Ivy League college and, believe it or not, this matters to the majority of my male client base. It's an option they have and they're exercising it. I could line you up with a dozen guys right now if I could change that one line item in your bio."

"Bonnie, are you serious? You want me to believe that the only reason you can't get me a date is because of where I went to college?"

"It's the truth."

"Let me get this straight… You try to pawn guys off on me that don't even come close to meeting my criteria, but you aren't willing to convince these dozen guys to go out with me when the only quality

I'm lacking, if you want to call it that, is that I didn't go to Harvard?"

"Victoria, the gentlemen don't have to settle. I have a pile of profiles sitting on my desk right now with the proper diplomas."

"Look, Bonnie, I appreciate your candor, but I don't have to settle either…and I won't. If you find a guy within the next ten months who is not repulsed by a gal with a state college education and someone who actually meets my requirements, call me. If I don't hear from you, well then, I guess I will have one more thing to chalk up to experience."

And, sure enough, ten months later the writing was on the blackboard—my $2,500 lesson from the School of Real Life, another non-Ivy League institution. ▨

And The
Award
Goes
To...

Mike is King of the Losers, Creeps, Jerks, and Weirdos, infamous award winner of the world title. Mike, if you are reading this, I have just two words for you: Karma, baby!

My date with Mike was another blind date setup (and, for the record, I gave up blind dating—for good—after this). The plan was to meet at 6 p.m. for drinks, with the possibility of dinner. It was March 12 and the location was a popular neighborhood pub. I arrived right on time; Mike showed up nearly 20 minutes late.

The first impression was a good one. He was tall and muscular with sandy blonde hair and aqua green eyes. He extended a pleasant greeting and then we quickly maneuvered through the crowd to secure two seats at the end of the bar.

I learned Mike was in broadcasting and had just recently landed a job as anchorman for a local news program. He was an avid sports enthusiast—football, basketball, baseball, soccer, you name it—and was the middle child in a family of seven.

The conversation didn't lag a bit and I was rather enjoying myself. Everything seemed to be going well; I hadn't paid attention to the time or, for that matter, anything else that was going on around me; I was completely tuned in to Mike. Mike finished his drink and excused himself to make a phone call. That's when I checked my watch—a mere 30 minutes had passed. I was thinking that when Mike returned I would propose that we grab a bite to eat.

A minute later, I caught sight of Mike gathering his jacket from coat check and heading toward the exit. I quickly took care of the tab and hurried after him.

"Mike...Mike! Wait up! Are you leaving?"

"I have to get going; I have to be somewhere."

"So you were just going to skip out?"

"Look, I have to go."

Mind you, Mike never once made eye contact; he just kept walking at a pace about five or six steps ahead of me. Once outside, he didn't bother to slow down. Standing at the top of the steps, I said in a loud enough voice to be heard by all in the immediate vicinity:

"Mike, what's going on here? Could you at least walk me to my car, please?"

At that, he stopped, turned around, and took a few steps back toward me—just close enough not to have to yell—"Victoria," he said "I'm used to dating prettier women. Okay?"

And that was that. Put a big fat period at the end of that sentence. He turned around, hopped in his fire red convertible, and sped out of the lot.

I'm not sure how long I stood there, but it had to have been a minute or two. I was absolutely stunned; and incredibly hurt. I wasn't Barbie, but I certainly wasn't Raggedy Anne. And, yes, everyone is entitled to their own opinion about what constitutes attractiveness, but to verbalize such an opinion in such a manner is, well, downright cruel.

So let's talk about ugly, shall we?—yes, let's talk about Mike! All together now, boys and girls, who is U-G-L-Y on the inside, where it counts? That's right—M-I-K-E!

On my drive home, I thought of a slew of cutting comebacks, but, frankly, they only provided temporary comic relief for my crushed ego. After I cried all the tears I had, I was left feeling tremendous pity for Mike. How sad to have a character so shamefully underdeveloped.

To Mike, there really are no words...

To my fellow sisters, be forewarned, Mike is out there somewhere swimming in the shallow end. ▨

Good Guys—
They
Really
Do
Exist

Ladies, let there be no mistake—good guys are hard to come by, but they do exist. When you have dated a swamp-full of toads, as I have, it is reasonable to buy into the opinion that all the good ones are taken or that all men are scum. Fortunately, neither is true. Like anything of great value, a good man is a real treasure and it takes a generous amount of patience, a little bit of luck, and a heck of a lot of frog interrogation to find the one.

When you are dating, consider yourself in the construction business. Not the type of construction that would have you building walls around yourself; but the kind that would have you work to strengthen your own areas of weakness. That's right, all those losers, creeps, jerks, and weirdos actually helped to make me a better person, and, in hindsight, I am able to see and appreciate the entertainment value they provided along the way. This is not to say that is has been easy and it certainly hasn't been without heartbreak, but, in the end, I know the reward will be worth it—for myself and for the person I decide to share a porch swing with.

Ross, or "Mac" as everyone calls him, is a good guy. Turns out Mac was in front of my eyes and living on the fringes of my life for several years before I actually saw him (read "noticed"). He is a few years older than me; divorced; a former athlete turned successful businessman; father of one; generous; centered; and wonderfully content with the simple things in life. He is handsome to be sure, but it was his intellect and ability to find the absurdity and humor in life's everyday adventures that eventually caught my attention and reeled in my heart.

Mac has taught me many things, the biggest lesson of which is how to live in the moment—one day at a time. We are friends first and foremost and I truly *like* him. There is no time clock, no pressure, and, quite significantly, we managed to maintain our individuality. We never had a desire to change one another or "couplize" everything in our lives. If one of us wanted to have a "solo weekend" it was available without risk of guilt, criticism, rejection, or resentment from the other. Love and caring were a by-product of our mutual respect—our relationship evolved gradually and naturally.

Everything was not peaches and cream, of course, and we had our share of "discussions" and moments when we were both glad to be single and able to call it a night. Good communication and a sense of humor were what always brought us through the rough patches.

So how does this story end?

Answer: With bad timing.

Not quite to the one-year milestone, Mac announced that his business necessitated he relocate to the Far East temporarily—three years "temporarily" to be precise. Yes, he asked me to go with him; and, yes, he knew the sacrifice that would require on my part; and, yes, he would understand my decision either way.

After a lot of talks and sleepless nights, I gave Mac my answer—No.

The good news is there are more great guys out there. Focus on your personal construction project, be patient, be open, and be thankful for the losers, creeps, jerks, and weirdos because without them you might not notice the good guy when you meet him.

As for Mac and I? I think he'd be lucky to share the porch swing with me and I with him. I guess we'll know in about three years. In the meantime, the search continues...

What's Your Dating Story?

To share your own losers, creeps, jerks, and weirdos dating story, please visit *www.HRHClassics.com*.

Quick Order Form

Fax Orders: 720-733-2341. Send this form.
Online Orders: *www.HRHClassics.com*
Postal Orders: HRHClassics, P.O. Box 261393
                     Highlands Ranch, CO 80163-1393

Please send _____ copies of *Losers, Creeps, Jerks, and
Weirdos: A Dating Story* (hard bound) @ $19.95 per copy
($29.95 Can) (+ sales tax and shipping as detailed below) to:

*(PLEASE PRINT. If shipping to more than one address, please
list additional addresses on separate sheet of paper.)*

Name: _____

Street Address: _____

City: _____ State: _____ Zip: _____

Telephone: _____ Country: _____

E-mail Address: _____

Sales Tax: Please add 4.7% if shipping to a Colorado address.

*Shipping: United States, add $4.00 for first book and $2.00 for
each additional book to same address.*

*International, add $9.00 for first book and $5.00 for each
additional book to same address.*

Payment: ☐ Check (payable to HRH Classics)
           ☐ Credit Card:
              ☐ Visa   ☐ MasterCard   ☐ AMEX

Card Number: _____

Name on Card: _____

Card Expires: _____

(Allow 4 weeks for delivery.)